PLAYSKOOL

Go Go Goes to the Doctor

by Samantha Brooke
illustrated by S. I. International

SIMON SPOTLIGHT
New York   London   Toronto   Sydney

To A. L.—I'll always go with you to the doctor.—S. B.

SIMON SPOTLIGHT
An imprint of Simon & Schuster Children's Publishing Division
1230 Avenue of the Americas, New York, New York 10020
HASBRO and its logo and PLAYSKOOL are trademarks of Hasbro and are used with permission.
© 2009 Hasbro. All Rights Reserved.
For information about special discounts for bulk purchases, please contact
Simon & Schuster Special Sales at 1-866-506-1949 or business@simonandschuster.com.
Manufactured in the United States of America
First Edition
2 4 6 8 10 9 7 5 3 1
ISBN 978-1-4169-8295-1

Go Go Dino opened up his mailbox. Inside was a postcard from Doctor Saurus. It said that Go Go should come for a visit.

Go Go showed his friends the postcard.
"Looks like you're supposed to go for a checkup," said Digger the Dog.
"What's a checkup?" asked Go Go.

"A checkup is a visit to the doctor when you're feeling good. It's so the doctor can make sure you're growing the right way," said Kitty Kandu. "I've had a checkup."

"Me too," said Tubby Turtle.

"Me three," said Digger the Dog.

"Was it scary?" asked Go Go.

"Maybe at first, but Doctor Saurus is really nice," said Kitty.

"Did you get a shot?" asked Go Go.

"Yes, but it only hurt for a moment," said Digger.

"I got a shot too," said Kitty Kandu. "But you'll be fine. I know you can do it!"

"Would you all come with me?" Go Go asked shyly.

"Of course we will!" said Tubby.

Go Go Dino and his friends walked to Doctor Saurus's office. "I have an idea," said Tubby. "Let's go to the playground after Go Go is done at Doctor Saurus's office. That way Go Go has something to look forward to." Everyone thought that was a great idea!

As Go Go and his friends waited for the doctor, they looked at books and played with toys.
"This doesn't seem so bad," thought Go Go.

After a little while Doctor Saurus came out and said, "Go Go, it's good to see you! Come on in."

Suddenly Go Go was nervous again.
"Can my friends come too?" he asked.
"Sure," said Doctor Saurus.

"First I'm going to weigh you, Go Go. Hop up on this scale," said Doctor Saurus.

Go Go got on the scale. Then the doctor said, "Your weight looks just fine for a dinosaur your age."

"Way to go, Go Go!" said Kitty Kandu.

"Now let's see how tall you are," said Doctor Saurus. She raised a bar until it touched the top of Go Go's head. "Also looks good," she said.

"This seems okay so far," thought Go Go.

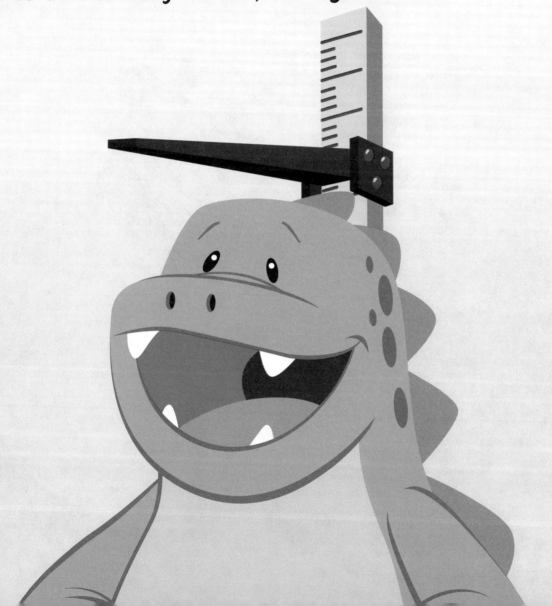

"Next I'm going to use a tool called a stethoscope to hear the sounds that your heart and lungs make," said Doctor Saurus. "Now take a deep breath for me."

Doctor Saurus gently moved the stethoscope over
Go Go's chest. Then she said, "Everything sounds fine."
"Way to go, Go Go !" said Tubby Turtle. Go Go smiled.

"Now I'm going to look in your ears, nose, and mouth with an otoscope," said Doctor Saurus.

Doctor Saurus looked in Go Go's ears and his nose. Then she said, "Can you stick out your tongue and say `ahh´?"

"Ahhhhh," said Go Go. Then he wiggled his tongue. That made everyone laugh.

"You're doing great, Go Go," said Doctor Saurus. "Now I'm going to test your reflexes with this little hammer."

"Will it hurt?" asked Go Go.

"No," said Doctor Saurus. "Just watch. I will make your legs jump all by themselves!"

Doctor Saurus gently tapped Go Go's knee, and his leg kicked out really fast.

Everyone laughed. "You've got great reflexes, Go Go," Doctor Saurus said.

"Way to go, Go Go!" said Digger.

"The last thing we need to do is give you an immunization," said Doctor Saurus. "It's like a shield that will protect you from getting sick."

"Cool!" said Go Go. "Is it something I wear?"

"This kind of shield goes on your insides.
It comes in a shot," said the doctor.
"Uh-oh," said Go Go.

"The shot will feel like a strong pinch, but should only hurt for a few seconds," said Doctor Saurus.
"Will you hold my hand, Kitty?" asked Go Go. "I'm scared."
"Of course," she said. "Squeeze it as hard as you need to."

"All right, Go Go. Count to five. When you're done counting, the shot will be over," said the doctor.
"One, two, three, four, five . . . ," said Go Go.

"Way to go, Go Go!" said Doctor Saurus. "And because you were so brave, I have something special for you."

Doctor Saurus gave Go Go Dino a sheet of stickers.

"Thanks, Doctor Saurus," said Go Go. "Come on, everyone, I'll race you to the playground!"